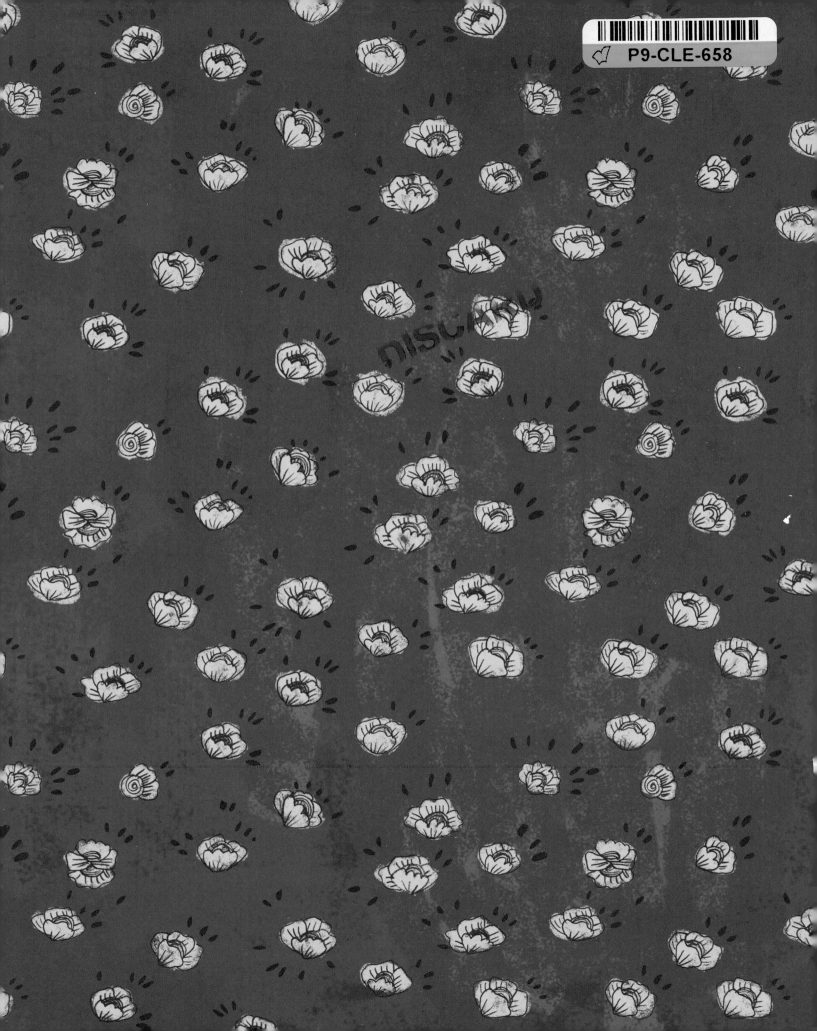

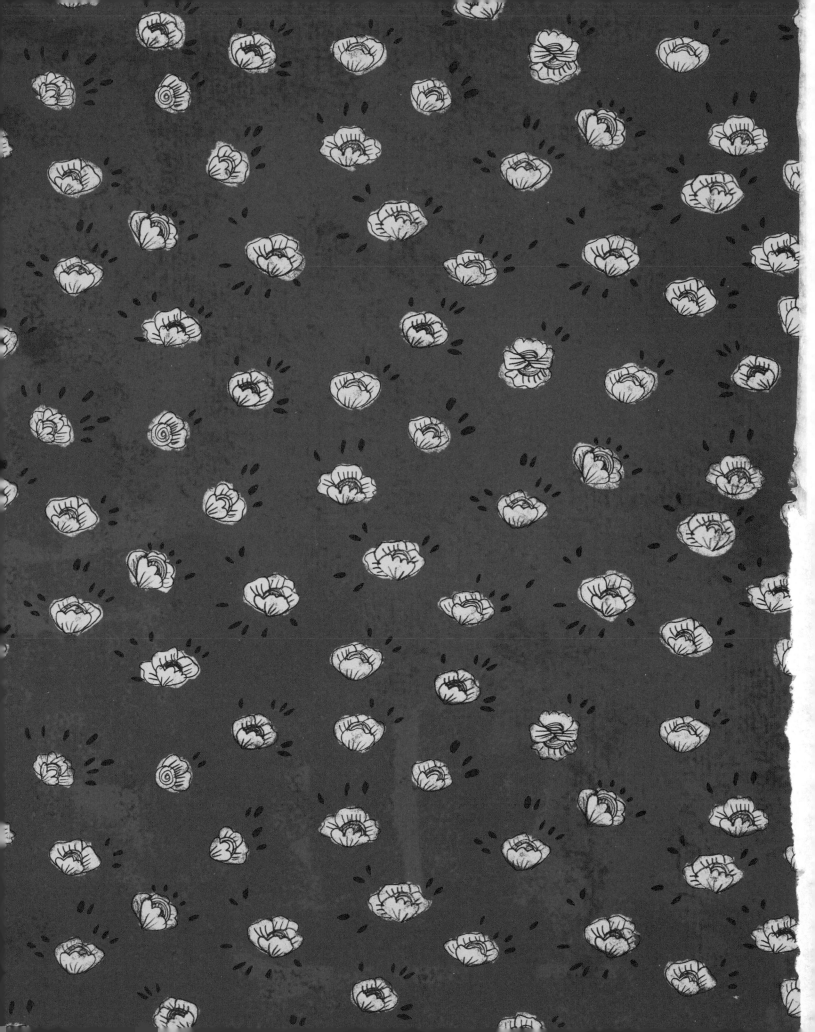

DINNER ON DOMINGOS

To my abuelita, Grandma Katona, my mom and all the people who work hard in the kitchen to bring everyone together — A. K.

To my mom, who makes the best food in the world. Thanks for making all our family gatherings so memorable — C. N.

Barefoot Books
23 Bradford Street, 2nd Floor
Concord, MA 01742

Barefoot Books
29/30 Fitzroy Square
London, W1T 6LQ

First published in the United States of America by Barefoot Books, Inc and in Great Britain by Barefoot Books, Ltd in 2021

Graphic design by Elizabeth Jayasekera, Barefoot Books
Edited and art directed by Lisa Rosinsky, Barefoot Books
Reproduction by Bright Arts, Hong Kong. Printed in China on 100% acid-free paper
This book was typeset in Barrio, Dear St. Nick, Mama Bear, Optima and Patrick Hand
The illustrations were prepared in graphite, pencils and digital techniques

Hardback ISBN 978-1-64686-293-1   Paperback ISBN 978-1-64686-294-8
E-book ISBN 978-1-64686-350-1

British Cataloguing-in-Publication Data:
a catalogue record for this book is available from the British Library

Library of Congress Cataloging-in-Publication Data
is available under LCCN 2021938515

1 3 5 7 9 8 6 4 2

DINNER ON DOMINGOS

written by **Alexandra Katona**

illustrated by **Claudia Navarro**

Barefoot Books
Step inside a story

Every Sunday, I head to
abuelita's casa for dinner
with mi familia.

My huge, extended family.

Before I'm even a step inside, here comes Blanco!

Then I'm hit by the smell of onions and garlic.
"Is abuelita making locro tonight?"
I love her potato soup.

La cocina is painted a bright cornflower blue.
Abuelita says it reminds her of the Ecuadorian sky.
Michigan is full of grey days and cold nights.

"¡Mija!" says abuelita.
She cups my face in her warm hands.
They smell like garlic.
"La comida siempre nos lleva a casa," she smiles.

I wish I had the words to answer.
"Food always leads us home," she translates
and sneaks me a taste of locro.

This kitchen is for cooking food
our grandmothers made us
and sautéing cebollas
and passing the phone around
to chat with faraway family.

One by one, my tíos and tías, primos and primas
burst through the door.
The house grows louder and louder.
Fuller and fuller. Kids laugh.
Dogs bark. Pots clang.

I run downstairs, where all my primos are playing.
It smells like mildew and fresh laundry.

"3, 2, 1, READY OR NOT, HERE I COME!"
shouts my primo Juan.

This basement is for mischievous plotting
and exploring dust-covered boxes
and making up new games with silly rules.

"¡ESTÁ LISTO!" shouts abuelita,
clapping through the noise.
    We all move quickly to the table, even the adults.
        She says una oración and always mentions abuelito:
            the love of her life.

This dining room is for remembering our loved ones
and blowing out birthday candles
and looking through tío Charlie's photo albums.

We spill over on couches and squish together.
We talk and tell jokes
and sneak Blanco a taste.

And when we dive in for more,
abuelita always smiles.
When we're full, her heart is too.

But sometimes,
we tease each other too much.
Emotions build and grow and expand,
until it feels like the room is going to explode.

"¡**BASTA!**" yells abuelita
when she's had enough,
with a stern face
and a sparkle in her eye.

Abuelita puts on a record
and it slowly starts to spin
around and around.

This living room is for piling presents
to the ceiling on Christmas Eve
and playing Lotería and board games
and spreading out blankets for cousin sleepovers.

Her calloused hand grabs mine.
Her feet bounce to the rhythm.
She leads — she always does.

My shoes keep finding their way on top of abuelita's feet.

"Lo siento," I confess in my American accent.

I wish I spoke more Spanish.

Abuelita raises her head to the sky and laughs,
making her bright eyes squint
and her round belly shake up and down.

Her hair tickles my eyes
and she kisses me on the forehead.
"Muy bien, Alejandra," she smiles.
She knows I'm trying.

I wrap my arms around abuelita's waist
and squish my face into the crook of her neck.
"¡Te quiero, abuelita!"
I say as best I can.

"Psst," whispers my
prima Dena into my ear
    and something shiny catches my eye.
        "KICK THE CAN!" we shout together.

I grab Dena's hand
    and we all rush out back to play,
    taking over the alley.

This home is for
pressing plátanos into tostones
    and feeding pájaros from the porch
    and celebrating new baby cousins.

Maybe, someday, I'll have grey hair and wisdom to share.
And a warm house with pots full of food,
a house hungry for memories.

Esta casa.

This magical home turns a normal Sunday into

DOMINGO: the best day of the week.

Author's Note

My mother was born in Quito, Ecuador, and moved to Pontiac, Michigan, with her growing family in 1955. They adjusted to being in America but were criticized for speaking Spanish and for being "different."

My mother's parents, my abuelos, spoke Spanish at home, but outside of it, my mother and her siblings tried to blend in — a familiar balancing act for many immigrants.

As I grew up, my mother did not teach me Spanish, but I longed to connect with my abuelos. Almost every Sunday, we would head to their house for dinner. Even though I didn't speak Spanish, those dinners helped connect us.

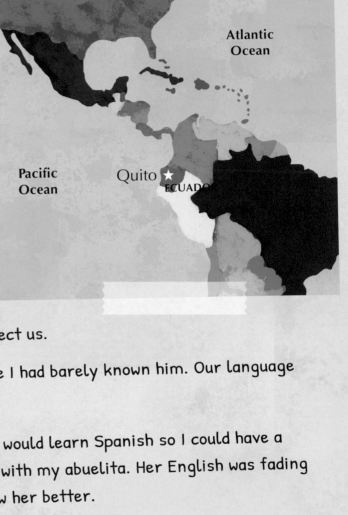

When I was 16, my abuelito passed away. I felt like I had barely known him. Our language barrier had created a rift I wanted to close.

I promised myself I would learn Spanish so I could have a better relationship with my abuelita. Her English was fading and I wanted to know her better.

I studied Spanish in high school and college. Then I went to Ecuador to live with my abuelita's sister for six months to better understand the language and her country.

While one of my grandmothers is Ecuadorian and the other was Sicilian, they both understood the power of eating a home-cooked meal together.

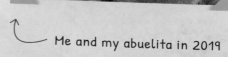

Me and my abuelita in 2019

Me and my cousins, scheming and arguing at the kitchen table

Abuelita in la cocina and abuelito hugging primo Juan in 1983

I am grateful for the sit-down dinners my mother prepared at home as well. Now, I make their recipes (including locro!) for my own family.

Abuelita is now 97 years old and can't hear or see all that well. We live over 2,000 miles apart, but I cherish our phone calls and video chats. Her smile still lights up the room and her advice remains true: live your life each and every day to the fullest.

abuelita [*ah-bweh-lee-tah*]: grandma

abuelito [*ah-bweh-lee-toh*]: grandpa

¡Basta! [*BAHS-tah*]: Enough!

cebollas [*seh-boy-ahs*]: onions

domingo [*doh-meeng-oh*]: Sunday

esta casa [*ehs-tah cah-sah*]: this house

"¡Está listo!" [*ehs-TAH lees-toh*]: It's ready!

la cocina [*lah coh-see-nah*]: the kitchen

La comida siempre nos lleva a casa [*lah coh-mee-dah syehm-preh nos yeh-vah ah cah-sah*]: Food always leads us home

Lo siento [*loh see-en-toh*]: I'm sorry

Lotería [*loh-teh-REE-ah*]: a card game similar to Bingo

mi familia [*mee fah-mee-lyah*]: my family

mija [*mee-hah*]: my daughter

muy bien [*mwee byehn*]: very good

pájaros [*PAH-hah-rohs*]: birds

plátanos [*PLAH-lah-nohs*]: plantains

prima [*pree-mah*]: girl cousin

primo [*pree-moh*]: boy cousin

¡Te quiero! [*teh kyer-oh*]: I love you!

tía [*tee-ah*]: aunt

tío [*tee-oh*]: uncle

una oración [*oo-nah oh-rah-SYOHN*]: a prayer

Abuelita's Recipe for
Traditional Ecuadorian LOCRO

Makes: 4 – 6 servings   Time: 1½ hours

Ingredients:

4 cups (900 mL) water

1½ – 2 lbs (680 – 900 g) potatoes, washed, peeled, diced and soaked in cold water (starchy varieties such as Russet or King Edward work best)

1 medium onion, chopped

3 or 4 cloves of garlic, finely chopped

½ tsp salt

1 cup (225 mL) milk

2 tsp achiote (or annatto) powder or ¼ tsp turmeric and/or ½ tsp sweet paprika

Salt and pepper to taste

1 cup (235g) cheese, grated (white cheese such as Monterey Jack or Cheddar works best)

To serve:

2 avocados, chopped

2 cups (470 g) lettuce, chopped (Romaine lettuce works well)

1 cup (235 g) tomatoes, chopped

Directions:

1. Add the water to a large pot and bring to a boil. Meanwhile, remove the potatoes from the cold water they're soaking in and rinse thoroughly.

2. Add the drained potatoes, onions and garlic to the boiling water.

3. Reduce to medium-low heat, add ½ tsp of salt, then cook for around 30 – 45 minutes or until the potatoes become very tender. While you're waiting, I suggest you have a dance party! (In between songs, check the potatoes.)

4. Once the potatoes are tender, use a wooden spoon to mash the potatoes slightly in the pot so that the soup becomes creamy. (Most of the potatoes will break down naturally.) Leave some chunks of potato as the different textures make it more interesting.

5. Reduce to a low heat, stir in the milk and the achiote powder then cook for a few more minutes. Add salt and pepper to taste. If the soup is too thick, add a bit more milk.

6. Remove the soup from the heat and stir in the cheese.

7. Immediately serve the soup into bowls. Add chopped avocado, lettuce and tomato on top.

8. Gather friends and family around the table and enjoy your meal together!

Alexandra Katona has been writing stories since she was young, but this is her debut picture book. When she's not writing, you can find her on an outdoor adventure or cooking for her family. She lives with her husband, son and dog in southern California, USA, and believes in the connective power of food.

Claudia Navarro has illustrated many books for children, including the critically acclaimed *La Frontera: El viaje con papá / My Journey with Papa* and *Dance Like a Leaf* for Barefoot Books. She says this story brought her back to her own childhood Sundays, when the whole family came over to enjoy her mother's cooking and all the kids ran around the house having fun together. Claudia lives in Mexico City, Mexico.